3 COYOTE TALES

Stories from the Sioux, Karok, and Zuni Indians

3 COYOTE TALES

Copyright © 2015 by Gini Graham Scott

TABLE OF CONTENTS

INTRODUCTION

The following three tales are adapted from stories told by the American Indians. They are drawn from some books I had long ago when I took classes on American Indian culture at San Francisco City College, and then I rewrote them.

I was intrigued by the stories of Coyote, the trickster figure in much of American Indian storytelling. He is always trying to fool people or get away with something; but his tricks catch up to him and his plans backfire. Yet he always returns to attempt more tricks. As such he is wily and clever, but not very wise. So he makes many mistakes – he is too smart for his own good.

The following Coyote stories come from the Sioux, Karok, and Zuni Indians.

The Sioux are a tribe from the Northwest, where they once formed the Great Sioux Nation. They have lived in the area that later became the states of North Dakota, South Dakota, Nebraska, Minnesota, Montana, and Wyoming.

The Karok are a tribe from Northwestern California, located along the Klamath River.

The Zuni are one of the Pueblo peoples, who have lived in villages in the area of New Mexico.

While these Indian tribes come from very different areas, their coyote stories are similar in the way Coyote has friends with other animals, participates with them on adventures, and screws things up no matter what he does.

Here are three of my favorite Coyote stories.

THE STORY OF COYOTE, BUFFALO, AND THE ROCK

An Adaptation of a Traditional American Indian Folktale

(Told by the Sioux Indians)

THE STORY OF COYOTE, BUFFALO, AND THE ROCK

    Coyote is one of the most popular characters in American Indian folktales. Sometimes he is wise and crafty and acts to help people. But often he plays tricks on others, which sometimes backfire, and he makes mistakes.

    This is a Coyote story told by the Sioux people of the Great Plains.

One day Coyote was walking along a path with his friend, Buffalo.

On the way, they passed a large rock, covered with green moss.

Coyote stopped, looked closely at the rock, and told Buffalo:

"I think this is a special rock. The lines on it tell a story. I think this rock has power."

"Yes," Buffalo agreed. "As I get closer, the rock feels warm, and I hear noises coming from the earth under it. So this must be a very powerful rock. It must be filled with the power of the earth and the Great Spirit."

Coyote took off the colorful woolen blanket he was wearing.

"I'd like to give this powerful rock a gift," he said to Buffalo.

He placed his blanket over the rock.

"Here, Rock, my friend, this is a present for you. It's a cold day, and this will keep you from freezing."

Buffalo gazed at Coyote with surprise. "What a big gift!" he said. "That was very generous of you."

Coyote flipped his tail. "It's not that much. I still have on my shirt to keep me warm. And I like giving things away. I think Rock looks very nice in my blanket."

"But now it's his blanket," said Buffalo.

Coyote and Buffalo continued their walk along the path.

Soon it began to rain. The rain came down harder and harder. The wind began to howl loudly through the trees. It got colder and colder. The rain turned to hail, and the path began to run with mud.

Coyote saw a cave ahead and bounded over to it to take refuge. Buffalo followed right behind him. But inside, cold water dripped from the top of the cave.

"I'm freezing," Coyote complained. He shivered and his teeth chattered. "You have your thick buffalo robe to keep you warm. But now I have only my light shirt."

The cold hail continued outside. The wind whipped even faster through the trees.

Shivering, his teeth chattering even more, Coyote turned to Buffalo and told him:

"Friend, I'm so cold and miserable now. Please go to Rock for me, since you have your warm coat and get me back my warm blanket. I need it now, and Rock really doesn't. After all, he has gotten along fine without a blanket for many years before I gave him one."

"All right," Buffalo agreed. "Since you are so cold, I will go. But I don't think you should do this. You gave your blanket as a gift."

"No, please go," Coyote urged, and Buffalo loped off.

Soon Buffalo came to Rock, who was covered by the colorful blanket Coyote had given him.

"Coyote would like his blanket back," Buffalo told Rock. "Can I have it?"

"No, I like this blanket," Rock replied firmly. "It has kept me dry and warm in this big storm. Besides, a gift is a gift. What's given is given."

So Buffalo returned to the cave and told Coyote: "Rock won't give the blanket back. He likes it because it keeps him dry and warm."

"What about me?" cried Coyote. "Besides, that was my blanket, and Rock did nothing to earn it. He didn't pay for the blanket. He didn't work for it. I just gave it to him. What an ungrateful rock. I'll go get the blanket back myself."

Coyote started running from the cave, when Buffalo called to him..

"Maybe you shouldn't go. Rock has a lot of power. I felt it coming from him. Maybe you should let him keep the blanket."

But Coyote shook his head. "No, that's stupid. The blanket I gave him is a very good expensive blanket, and it's very thick and warm. Now it's so cold. I'll go talk to Rock and explain why I need it back."

Soon Coyote saw Rock and his blanket on the path. He stopped before him.

"Let me have my blanket back now," Coyote said. "Why won't you give it back? You don't really need it, and I do, because it is now so cold and wet."

But Rock replied firmly: "No, I like this blanket. Besides, what's given is given."

Coyote's eyes reddened with anger. "You terrible rock. Can't you see I'm freezing and could catch my death of cold?"

Coyote reached out and grabbed the blanket. "Then, I'll take it back myself."

Coyote threw the blanket over his shoulders. "Now, that's that; over and done with."

He turned and bounded away.

"Well, maybe not," Rock called after him. "Maybe not."

Coyote ignored Rock and loped back to the cave. On the way, the rain stopped and the sun began shining brightly.

"I'm warm again," Coyote thought happily.

Soon he was back at the cave. Buffalo joined him outside, since it was sunny and warm once more. They lay relaxing in the sun for a few hours.

Then, Coyote made a fire and cooked a meal with corn bread and soup made from berries.

After dinner, as they smoked their tobacco pipes and told stories, Buffalo's ears suddenly perked up.

"What's that funny noise?" he asked.

Coyote raised his head and twisted his ears around in every direction.

"I don't hear a thing," he said.

But Buffalo felt the ground start to shake under his feet, and he kept listening.

"No, no. There is something. Listen. It's a crashing and rumbling sound. It's very far off, but it's getting louder."

Coyote again raised his head high and twisted his ears around. Finally, he heard the noise.

"It sounds like thunder," he said.

As the sound got louder and louder, Coyote became frightened.

"The ground is beginning to shake like an earthquake," he cried. "Whatever can this be?"

Before Buffalo could answer, they saw a cloud of dust coming down the path. In the center of the cloud, they saw the big rock bouncing and crashing along.

"He's heading right for us," screamed Buffalo.

"It looks like he's trying to kill us," yelled Coyote. "Quick. Let's get away."

The two turned and ran as fast as they could. But the rock kept rolling and thundering after them.

"It's getting closer and closer," Coyote howled with fear. "Whatever shall we do?"

Suddenly, Buffalo noticed they were approaching a river.

"Let's swim across," he suggested. "Surely Rock can't swim after us, because he is so heavy."

They jumped in and began swimming. But the rock rolled into the river a few yards behind them and floated across, like a big wooden box.

So Coyote and Buffalo swam even harder.

Finally, they dragged themselves onto the shore. Coyote noticed a stand of pine trees ahead of them.

"Let's go there," he cried to Buffalo. "Surely Rock can't follow us there. The trees are so close together."

So Coyote and Buffalo ran into the forest.

But the rock rolled even faster after them. It rolled so fast, it tore a hole in the tree trunks as it sped through.

Now, with the rock just a few feet behind them, Coyote and Buffalo ran from the forest onto the plains.

Buffalo yelled out at Coyote: "I'm tired of running, and this isn't my fight anyway. Rock is angry at you, not me. So I'm going to say goodbye."

With that, Buffalo kicked up a big ball of dust and rolled himself into a little ball. Then, he turned into a spider, crawled into a mouse hole, and disappeared.

Coyote ran on alone. He felt the ground shake even harder under his feet, as the rock came closer and closer. The sound behind him was like a huge thunderstorm and earthquake.

"Oh, no. No. Please, don't" shrieked Coyote.

But it was too late. In the next moment, the rock rolled over him and flattened him out like a pancake.

Then, Rock picked up the blanket and rolled off, saying: "Well, now I have <u>my</u> blanket back again. So, goodbye. I'm going home."

Coyote lay on the ground for several hours, stunned and too sore to move.

At dusk, a rancher on a horse passed by. He saw Coyote still flat on the ground and stopped.

"What a nice-looking rug," he said aloud.

He got off his horse, picked up Coyote, and draped him over his saddle. Then, he rode home with his new rug.

Once home, the rancher put Coyote, still flat as a rug, in front of his fireplace. He lit the fire to warm up the house and went to bed.

As the rancher and his wife slept, the warmth of the fire warmed up Coyote, and he began to come back to life. For that's the way Coyote is. He may be killed, but afterwards, he can bring himself back to life.

So, as the night wore on, Coyote wriggled, stretched, and sucked in lots of air to puff himself up into his usual shape.

In the morning, Coyote was his old self. He got up and waited quietly by the fireplace until the rancher's wife opened the kitchen door. Then, he scurried out quickly and disappeared, running across the plains in a whirl of dust.

After that, Coyote never tried to get his blanket back from the rock, since he had learned his lesson -- at least for awhile -- that true generosity is a gift of the heart and a gift once given should be given forever. For that was the lesson of the rock.

HOW COYOTE BECAME CLEVER

An Adaptation of a Traditional American Indian Folktale

(Told by the Karok Indians)

Among the American Indians, Coyote is widely known as a clever trickster. He plays many tricks on people to get his way and help others, and sometimes he is successful. But sometimes he is fooled by his own tricks.

The American Indians have many stories about how Coyote gained his cleverness. This is one told by the Karok people of Northern California.

When the god of creation created the world and the animals, he made the animals equal in power and rank. All were equal -- the fishes in the ocean, the bears in the mountains, the buffalo on the plains, the deer in the forest, and every other animal.

Coyote was just like all the others.

After creating all the animals, the god of creation made a human being. He decided to ask this human to help him decide which animals should have the most and least power.

One day, when this man walked in the mountains, the god of creation appeared to him in a vision and told him:

"Make a bow and arrow of different lengths for each animal. When you are finished, I will ask all the animals to come together, and you will give these bows and arrows to them. Decide which animals should have the most power and give them the longest bows and arrows. Decide which ones should have the least power, and give them the shortest bows and arrows."

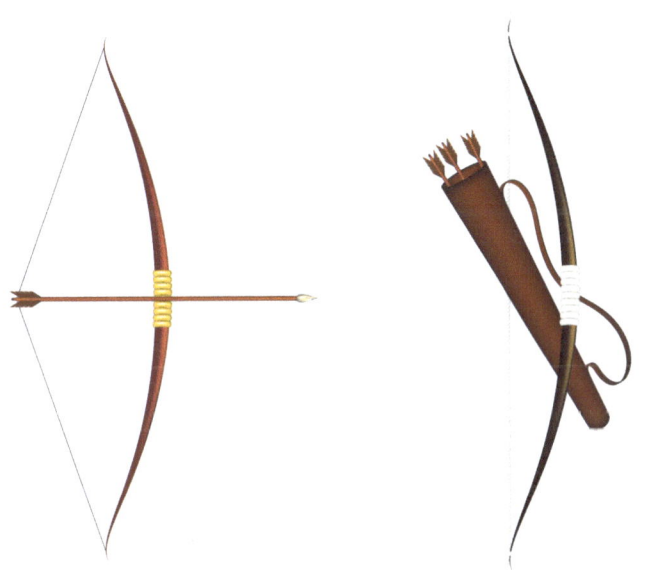

The man walked back to his village and began to make bows and arrows. He cut down the branches of hundreds of birch and fir trees. For the next ten days, he worked away, turning these branches into bows and arrows. Finally, he was done.

Now the god of creation asked all the animals to meet together in the forest. They came from far and wide. Even the fishes swam along the streams to the meeting.

As the animals gathered in a circle, the god of creation told them:

"Tomorrow a man will come to give you each a bow and arrow. The animal who gets the longest bow will have the most power. The one with the shortest bow will have the least power."

Then, in a flash of light, the god of creation was gone.

The animals got ready to go to sleep for the night. Bear found a dark cave. Deer found a soft pile of leaves. Buffalo found some grass. The fishes rested in the water. The other animals found resting places, too.

Coyote decided to trick the others by staying awake all night. This way, he thought: "I can be the first to meet the man in the morning. Then I can get the longest bow, so I will have the most power."

The other animals settled down for the night and went to sleep. But Coyote only pretended to do so. He made a nest of leaves and lay down in it.

But he kept his eyes open.
"I won't fall asleep," he said to himself.

As the night wore on and it got darker, Coyote began to feel sleepy. He felt his eyes start to close, and he shook himself.

"No, I won't fall asleep," he said.

But he only got sleepier and sleepier and shook himself some more.

About midnight, he got up and walked around.

"Maybe this will keep me awake," he said.

He rubbed his eyes again and again to keep them open. But he felt sleepier and sleepier.

"What else can I do to stay awake?" he wondered.

He hopped up and down on one foot. He jumped ahead as far as he could. The exercise woke him up.

But some of the animals called out to him: "Don't do that. You're waking us up."

So he had to stop.

Next he tried to talk to himself to stay awake. But when the first light of dawn appeared in the East, he was so tired, he couldn't keep his eyes open any longer.

What could he do?

Suddenly, Coyote had an idea.

"I'll keep my eyes propped open with some sticks."

He looked around, found two small sticks, and sharpened the ends against a stone. Then, he placed the sticks against his eyelids and the bottom of each eye to keep his eyes open.

"Now I can go to sleep safely," Coyote told himself. "I can keep my eyes open to watch the sun rise. Then, I can get up before it's completely light and the other animals get up."

Coyote lay down on his nest of leaves to get a few minutes sleep. In a few seconds, he was fast asleep.

At once, his eyes snapped shut, for the sharp ends of the sticks pierced his eyelids. Instead of keeping his eyes open, the sticks sealed them shut.

Coyote fell into a deep, deep sleep.

When the other animals got up, Coyote was still sleeping. He even snored loudly.

The other animals laughed as they passed by on their way to meet the man to get their bows. He was waiting for them in a large clearing with a big pile of bows around him.

The animals formed a circle around him. He glanced about to decide who should get each bow.

"I'll give you the longest bow," he told Cougar, "because you live high in the mountains."

"I'll give you the next-longest bow," he told Bear, "Because you are so strong."

Then, the man continued around the circle, giving a bow to each animal.

Finally, he had only one bow left -- the very shortest. The man looked around the circle.

"Who didn't get a bow yet?" he asked.

The animals looked about. Every animal there had a bow.

Suddenly, Mouse cried out: "I know who's missing. It's Coyote. We passed him sleeping in his nest."

All the animals began laughing.

"Yes, yes," they cried out. "It is Coyote."

Then, leaping, running, and hopping, they led the man to Coyote's nest. Coyote was still snoring heavily, and his eyes were sealed tightly shut by the two sticks in his eyelids.

"You truly deserve the shortest bow," the man said. "You have slept through our meeting."

He pulled the sticks out of Coyote's eyes and handed him the shortest bow.

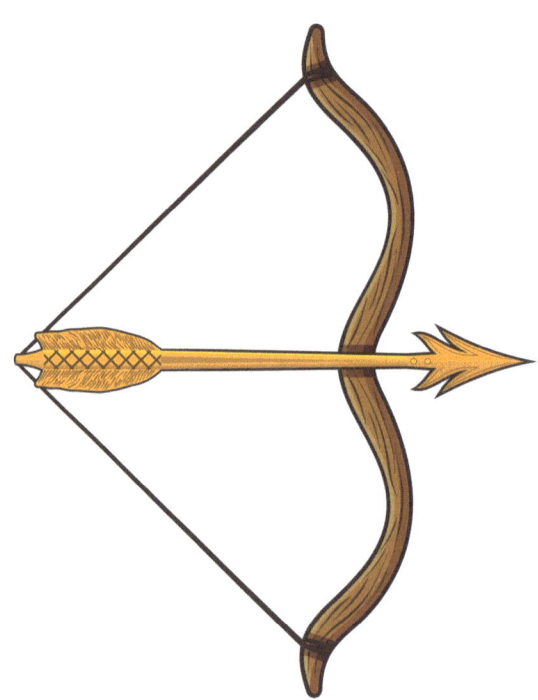

As Coyote rubbed his very sore eyes and took the bow, the other animals laughed loudly.

Bear gave a great big roar. Buffalo stomped up and down.

Deer kicked up his heels. Even Mouse cackled and shrieked with laughter.

So the man felt very sorry for Coyote, who would now be the weakest animal of all.

That night in his prayers, the man told the creator he was sorry for Coyote.

"Can't you do something to help him? He is so weak now," he prayed.

The creator heard him and replied: "Yes, I will help him. I will make him more clever than the other animals."

And that's how Coyote became the cleverest of them all.

HOW COYOTE BROUGHT WINTER INTO THE WORLD

An Adaptation of a Traditional American Indian Folk Tale

(Told by the Zuni Indians)

For the American Indians Coyote is many things. Sometimes he is a trickster who fools people or gets fooled by his own tricks. Sometimes he is a creator, who brings things to help the Indian people. Sometimes, he does mischievous things.

This is one story which the Indian people tell about the Coyote and how his mischief created winter.

One day long ago when the world was still dark and there was no sun and moon, Coyote was out hunting. But he couldn't catch anything. He chased rabbits, but they ran too fast. He chased gophers, but they ran into their holes. He ran after a squirrel, but it scampered away.

He noticed Eagle hunting rabbits. Eagle swooped down and caught one rabbit after another.

"He has more rabbits than he can eat," Coyote thought.

"Maybe if I hunt with Eagle, I'll be more successful and have enough to eat."

So Coyote climbed to Eagle's nest in the mountains and asked him: "Why don't we hunt together? Then, we can both catch more game. Two are better than one."

"Gladly," Eagle agreed. "That sounds like a good idea."

Coyote and Eagle went out in the darkness to hunt the next day. Eagle whirled and swooped in the air, while Coyote ran quietly on the ground.

Again and again, Eagle flew to the ground and each time caught a rabbit. But many times, Coyote darted after what sounded like a rabbit running in the grass. But when he got there, the rabbit was gone.

At the end of the day, Eagle proudly showed of his dozen rabbits. But Coyote had nothing to show.

Coyote felt badly about his poor showing. He went to see Eagle in the mountains again to explain:

"I couldn't catch anything, because it was so dark, and I can't see well in the dark. You can. I need the light to see. Do you know where we can get some?"

Eagle look around from his high perch. He looked to the east, to the north, to the south, and finally to the west.

"I think I see a little light there," Eagle said. He pointed to a slight yellow glow on the western horizon. "We can go there to try to find it."

They set off to find the light. Eagle flew in the air above Coyote leading the way.

They crossed through the desert and went over a mountain.

They passed through a valley.

Then they came to a river. Eagle flew right over. Coyote jumped in and started to swim. Suddenly, he felt himself being pulled under by the current. He paddled furiously with his legs.

Eagle could only watch helplessly.

"I can't lift you in my wings. You are too heavy," he said.

Finally, coughing and spitting up water, Coyote pulled himself out on the other side of the river. He lay on the bank gasping.

"I almost drowned," he sputtered. "I wish I could fly across like you. But you have wings and feathers. I just have a coat of hair."

After Coyote rested, they continued on.

At last, they came to a small Indian village, called a pueblo. They passed by a dozen houses made of baked clay.

In the center of the village, they saw a dozen dancers in bright feathers dancing by a fire. These were the Kachina dancers, performing the sacred dances of the tribe.

About 50 Indians gathered around them watching the ceremony. The chief came over to welcome Coyote and Eagle.

"Come join us and watch the dancers," he said.

Coyote and Eagle sat down, and an Indian woman brought them some corn to eat.

As they watched, Eagle commented: "These dancers have much power. I think these people must have the light we are seeking."

Coyote glanced around. He noticed that two of the dancers each held a box. One box was large, the other small. From time to time, he saw the dancers open these boxes and the light inside lit up the dance.

When one dancer opened the big box, which held the sun, the light shone very brightly. When the other dancer opened the small box, which held the moon, there was only a little light.

Coyote turned excitedly to Eagle, saying: "Look at those boxes. We don't have to go any further now. These dancers have all the light we need in their big box. Let's steal it and take it home with us."

Eagle hesitated. "Let's not steal it. Let's just ask to borrow the box," he suggested.

Coyote shook his head. "No. Why should they lend it to us? We will have to steal it to get it."

Finally, Eagle agreed. "All right. If that is the only way. Let's get it when they finish dancing."

After several hours, the Kachina dancers and other people went home to sleep.

"Now we can steal the box," Coyote said.

Eagle flew over to the box, scooped it up in his large claws, and flew off with it. Coyote ran along below him, trying to keep up.

Soon Coyote was panting for breath and called to Eagle.

"Slow down and let me carry the box for a while."

Eagle shook his head. "No, no. You never do anything right. You couldn't catch any rabbits, and you almost drowned in the river."

So Eagle flew on, and Coyote continue to run after him, gasping for breath.

A few hours later, Coyote called to Eagle again.

"Please let me carry the box. If I don't, people will think I'm lazy."

Again Eagle refused, saying: "No, no. You always do things wrong." Then, he flew on and Coyote still followed.

After a few more hours, Coyote begged again.

"Please, please, let me carry the box. It's not right for you to carry it all the way. What will people think of us?"

This time Eagle replied: "All right. I can't stand all your pestering."

Eagle flew down and handed the box to Coyote.

"Now you must promise not to open this," he warned.

Coyote nodded. "Yes. I promise."

Then, Eagle flew on as before, with Coyote following.

After a while, Coyote became very tired, because the box was heavy. He ran more and more slowly, while Eagle flew further and further ahead.

Finally, Coyote stopped to rest behind a hill where Eagle couldn't see him. As he rested, Coyote glanced at the box beside him.

"I wonder what the light in there looks like," he thought to himself.

He started to lift the lid. But he quickly put it back down, because he remembered his promise to Eagle not to open it.

Then, he thought to himself: "I wonder why this box is so heavy. Maybe there's something extra in this box, which Eagle doesn't want to tell me about. Maybe he wants to keep this special good thing for himself."

So Coyote picked up the box again and turned it around in his paws.

"Why not look?" he said finally. "Then I can see for myself what's there."

So Coyote opened the box.

Inside, he saw the bright golden ball of the sun. Its glow was brilliant and lit up the meadow. Next to it, he saw the smaller and not as bright silver ball of the moon.

Eagle had put the sun and the moon together in one box, because he thought it would be easier to carry them this way.

Coyote began to close the box again. But before he could shut it completely, the moon jumped out and began to roll away.

Coyote ran after the moon to catch it and put it back. But the moon was too fast for him. It rolled ahead faster and faster. Then it flew up into the sky. As it climbed higher and higher, all the plants dried up and became brown. The leaves dropped off of the trees.

Coyote leaped up to grab the moon. But the moon rose higher and higher, and he couldn't jump high enough to reach it.

Meanwhile, as Coyote tried to catch the moon, the sun jumped out of the box, too. It rolled along the ground and rose up into the sky.

Coyote raced back and leaped up to stop the sun. But the sun rose higher and higher, and drifted further and further away to the other side of the world.

As the sun disappeared in the distance, the fruit and vegetables in the gardens began to shrivel up from the cold. The corn, squashes, peaches, and melons all began to die.

For now it was winter, and it had become very cold.

Eagle wondered what happened to Coyote, and he turned back. As he flew closer, he noticed that all the plants had become brown and there were no leaves on the trees. He saw the shriveled up corn, squashes, peaches, and melons. And he felt it growing colder and colder.

Below him, Eagle saw Coyote next to the open box. He flew down and landed beside him.

"You fool," he yelled at Coyote. "You opened the box and let the sun and the moon escape."

Just then, it began to snow, and Coyote shivered. His teeth began to chatter.

Eagle continued. "So now it's cold. It's winter. You have let cold and winter into the world by what you have done."

And that's how Coyote brought winter into the world. He was too curious and tricky for his own good.

ABOUT THE AUTHOR

Gini Graham Scott has published over 50 books with mainstream publishers, focusing on social trends, work and business relationships, and personal and professional development. Some of these books include *The Very Next New Thing*, *The Talk Show Revolution*, *The Privacy Revolution*, *The Battle for Personal Privacy*, and *Fantasy Worlds*.

She has gained extensive media interest for previous books, including appearances on *Good Morning America, Oprah, Montel Williams, CNN,* and hundreds of radio interviews. She has frequently been quoted by the media and has set up websites to promote her most recent books at www.ginigrahamscott.com and www.changemakerspublishingandwriting..com. As of this writing, she has about 75,000 listings in Google Search Results.

She has become a regular Huffington Post blogger since December 2012, and has a Facebook page featuring her books and films at www.facebook.com/changemakerspublishing.

She has written, produced, and sometimes directed over 60 short videos, which are featured on her Changemakers Productions website at www.changemakersproductions.com and on YouTube at www.youtube.com/changemakersprod.

Her screenplays, mostly in the drama, crime, legal thriller, and sci-fi genres, include several that consider the social implications of science and technological breakthroughs and changes in society, including *The New Child, New Identity, Dead No More, Tax Revolt,* and *The Suicide Party.* All of these are in development with trailers, business plans, and interested directors and talent.

She has a PhD in sociology from U.C. Berkeley and MAs in anthropology, pop culture and lifestyles, recreation and tourism, and organizational/consumer/audience behavior from Cal State, East Bay. She is getting an MA in communications in June 2016.

She is also the Creative Director of Publishers, Agents and Films (www.publishersagentsandfilms.com), a service which connects writers to publishers, agents, and the film industry.

Her feature film, SUICIDE PARTY: SAVE DAVE, which she wrote and executive produced, is being released in the summer of 2015. Details are at www.suicidepartyfilm.com.

Additional bio and promotional material is at her websites at www.ginigrahamscott.com and www.changemakerspublishingandwriting.com.

CHANGEMAKERS PUBLISHING
3527 Mt. Diablo Blvd., #273
Lafayette, CA 94549
changemakers@pacbell.net . (925) 385-0608
www.changemakerspublishingandwriting.com

Featuring Photos from the Dollar Photo Club